WITHDRAWN

Pat Hutchins

Greenwillow Books
An Imprint of HarperCollinsPublishers

Don't Forget the Bacon!
Copyright © 1976 by Pat Hutchins
All rights reserved. Manufactured in China
For information address HarperCollins Children's
Books, a division of HarperCollins Publishers,
10 East 53rd Street, New York, NY 10022.
www.harperchildrens.com

Library of Congress Cataloging-in-Publication Data
Hutchins, Pat
   Don't forget the bacon! / by Pat Hutchins.
      p.   cm.
   "Greenwillow Books."
   Summary: A little boy goes grocery shopping for his mother and tries hard to
remember her instructions.
   ISBN 0-688-80019-X — ISBN 0-688-84019-1 (lib. bdg.)
   ISBN 0-688-06787-5 (1987 Printing)
   ISBN 0-688-06788-3 (lib bdg. 1987 Printing) — ISBN 0-688-08743-4 (pbk.)
   [1. Stories in rhyme]   I. Title.
PZ8.3.H965Do   75-17935
[E]   CIP
                                                                          AC

12 13 SCP 20 19 18 17

For Ben and Jeb Kidd